Diego Rivera

An Artist's Life

Written by Sarah Vázquez

STECK-VAUGHN
ELEMENTARY · SECONDARY · ADULT · LIBRARY

A Harcourt Classroom Education Company

www.steck-vaughn.com

 **Contents**

His Youth

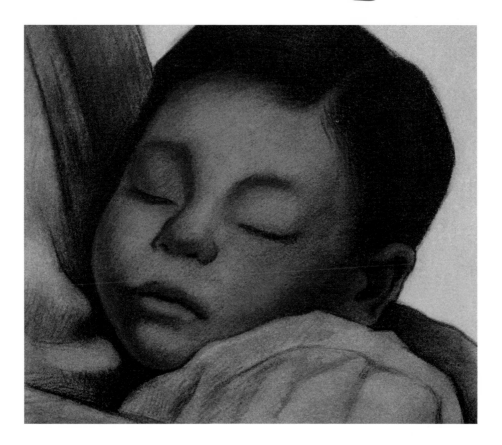

Diego Rivera was born in 1886 in a town called Guanajuato. It is high in the mountains of Mexico. Diego had a **twin** brother named Carlos. His parents were very happy when the twins were born. Their other babies had died.

Diego Rivera was named after his father. His father worked as a teacher. He also visited other schools to make sure they were teaching the children well. Diego's parents helped poor people. His parents wanted everyone to have a better life.

Diego's paintings show the people and land of Mexico.

Diego loved toy trains. One of his favorite things to do was to take them apart. He wanted to see how trains worked.

Diego also loved to draw. He began drawing when he was just three. He liked to draw trains. He drew everywhere he could reach. He drew on the chairs, on the walls, on the floor, or on paper.

Diego painted this girl playing with blocks.

Diego spent much of his time drawing. Sometimes he drew on the walls of his bedroom. His parents didn't want him to draw there, so they covered the walls in his room with plain paper. Then Diego was free to draw on his walls. That is how he painted his first wall paintings. These wall paintings are called **murals.**

Many people go to see Diego Rivera's murals.

Diego the Student

When Diego was ten years old, he started using paints to add colors to his drawings. Then he decided to be a painter. His parents let him take art classes after school.

After high school, young Diego went to the San Carlos School of Fine Arts. There he learned to love the art of the Mexican Indians. Their art showed the land, people at work, and their animals.

This Rivera painting shows Mexican Indians at work.

Diego learned many lessons from his teacher. Diego's teacher had a shop in Mexico City. He drew **cartoons** that made people laugh. He liked to draw poor people as being very good and rich people as being bad.

Diego began to paint this way, too. In 1906, some of his paintings were put in an art show. He began to sell his paintings to earn money. His paintings sold well.

In this painting, Diego shows doctors helping others.

Diego the Painter

Diego Rivera wanted to learn more about painting. He went to Europe in 1907 to study. He tried many different painting **styles.** He liked paintings that showed real people in real places. He did not like the modern styles where things did not look real.

In 1921, Diego went back to Mexico. He painted a mural for a school. He showed many Indian people in this mural. He painted with bright, strong colors. The shapes were large and simple. This was his own style.

Diego also used many pieces of colored glass to make murals. They are called **mosaic** murals.

This mosaic mural by Diego Rivera has many bright colors.

His Marriage

In 1928, Diego met an **artist** named Frida Kahlo. She was in art school, and Diego was painting a mural there. She went to see him to ask him about her paintings. They became friends and got married a year later. In the following years, they became famous together.

Frida had been in pain much of her life. Frida had polio as a child and was in a bus wreck in her teens. While she was ill, she taught herself to paint. She painted many **self-portraits.**

This is a self-portrait by Frida Kahlo.

 **His Later Years**

In 1931, there was an art show in New York City with 150 of Diego's paintings. Many other artists came to study with him. He became famous for his style of painting murals. He liked painting

This is one wall of the huge murals in Detroit.

pictures that could be seen by many
people in **public** places.

In 1932, the City of Detroit hired
Diego for a huge job. He painted 27
murals on four walls of the Detroit
Institute of Arts.

In 1933, Diego was hired to paint a mural by a man in New York City. But when the man saw the people in the mural, he did not like one person shown. He asked Diego to change it, but Diego would not. After Diego was paid, the man had the mural painted over. Later, Diego painted a smaller mural of this scene in Mexico City.

After that, Diego had hard times for a while. He lost some jobs in the United States. He didn't sell as much there. But he kept busy painting in Mexico.

Diego Rivera worked in this studio.

In 1950, Diego Rivera won Mexico's National Art Prize. His country held a big party for him on his seventieth birthday. But in 1955, he became ill, and he died a year later.

Diego Rivera's art lives on. Many of his paintings and murals are in **museums** all around the world. Some of his best murals can be seen in the National Palace in Mexico City. Because of his beautiful artwork, people will always remember Diego Rivera.

Diego loved to paint people.

 # Glossary

artist person who paints or draws

cartoons drawings done in a way to make people laugh

mosaic picture made up of many small pieces of glass

murals wall paintings

museums places where art is shown

public open to anyone

self-portraits paintings an artist draws of himself or herself

styles different ways of doing something

twin brother or sister born the same day